The Brave Mermaid

Mermaid Kariel and her Baby by Alicia Franco

The Brave Mermaid

A story to celebrate talents, and help
kids gain self confidence.

Volume One of "Kariel's Inspirational Mermaid Series".

Written and Illustrated by Mermaid Kariel

The Brave Mermaid
By: Mermaid Kariel
Copyright ©2010 by Mermaid Kariel
Library of Congress Control Number: 2014930274

Thank you for supporting the hard work of this author and purchasing a book to help make a difference in the lives of children.

Photography on front and back cover of Mermaid Kariel by Alicia Franco.

www.MermaidKariel.com

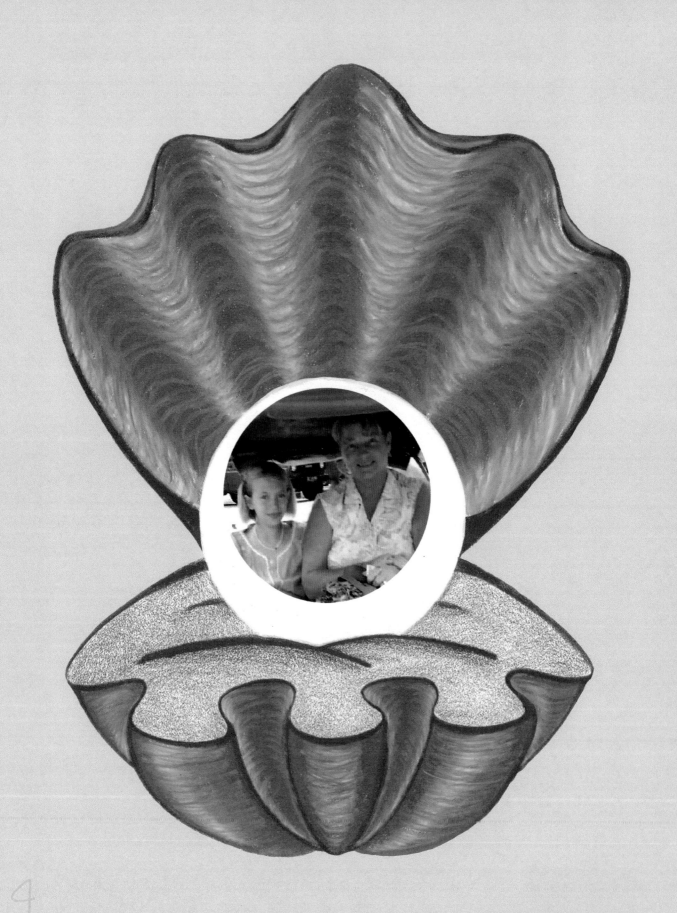

4

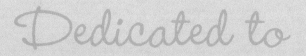
Dedicated to

Dedicated to Dorothy D. Clayton.

My hero, my Grandmother. For leading by example to

always treat others with kindness. Sharing with me your

emotional strength, unconditional love and elegance in

the way you lived your life. Every day I honor you and

teach my daughter and students the way of your love.

Thank you for blessing my life.

Aloha! My name is Mermaid Kariel and I want to tell you a story about my home. I live in the Pacific Ocean near the Hawaiian Islands! You have to swim really fast and go very deep to get to my underwater city where the ocean is warm and the Mer people live. The water becomes clear and very easy to see through.

There are many beautiful sea flowers and coral reefs. Next to the most beautiful sea garden of all lives a pink mermaid known as Momma Mermaid. She has three Mer children. Her oldest daughter is Mashell, who is known to be very quiet. Her two younger daughters, Double and Trouble, are known as the twins who have loud tantrums! They are always arguing and whining. Do you know what whining sounds like?

"Floppy is mine," Double would say. *"NOOOOOO! Floppy Fishy is mine,"* Trouble would whine back.

Momma Mermaid always has her fins full. You can tell that she is tired by the look of her dull, color-drained tail.

Mashell has a secret place, behind the sea garden, to escape

to when Double and Trouble whine. She has the best time

singing and dancing there. She calls her secret place the

"Echo Cave". She loves to go in her Echo Cave and sing as

loud as her gills let her. *"La La La La!"*

One day, Mashell was singing, splashing, and dancing around,

when suddenly, she started to feel as if she weren't alone.

What or who do you think was watching her?

Standing before her was Mer Rad Chad. Rad Chad is known for for his beautiful sea gardens and coral reefs. He has a green tail! He can make anything grow. Rad Chad's flowers make the whole sea happy. Many of the flowers in my city look like the same flowers you can find in the Hawaiian Islands. Hibiscus that are big and beautiful, Plumerias that smell sweet and Birds of Paradise that are as colorful as parrot fish! Have you seen these flowers before?

"Wow, was that you singing?" asked Rad Chad. Mashell looked at the sea floor as she hung her head with embarrassment and quietly replied, "Yes."

"Amazing. You SHOULD NOT be shy that I heard you sing," said Rad Chad in a matter of fact sort of way.

Bashfully, Mashell replied, "Oh, but I am. I never sing in front of other people. I don't want them to think I sound like I am whining or yelling. I really don't want to bother Mer people, or even worse, for them to laugh at me."

"Why under the sea would you think that? You sound like an angel fish. It's a talent to sing! Talents are meant to be shared with the world! Everyone has their own special talent. My talent is gardening. If you share your talent, I bet you will make your family really happy."

"I know a way you can be brave and believe in yourself. It's as easy as 1, 2, 3, 4. Follow me," explained Mer Rad Chad.

1. Place your hand over your heart.

2. Now grab all the hurtful things off your heart.

3. Throw your arm to the side as you open your hand and let go of all the hurtful things you were holding onto.

4. Now say "Swish" and shine bright like a star fish!

Can you say "Swish" and throw all the hurtful things off your heart? You can do it loud or you can say it soft. You can do it secretly or you can show it off.

Mashell sat on a bubble and thought very hard about what Mer Rad Chad was explaining to her. *"Wow, thank you Chad. I never thought of my voice as special or a talent. I know I love singing, but I hadn't thought that others would like it too!"* Mashell said with joy and excitement.

Do you know what a talent is? It's something very special that you can do! Everyone has a talent. It could be anything: gymnastics, solving math problems in your head, singing or gardening. Talents are meant to be shared with others! Have you ever smelled flowers or been given flowers? Did they make you feel happy? Did you think they smelled nice? Now imagine if Rad Chad or other gardeners never shared their flowers. Your talent will make someone happy, and that's why you should share it! What is your talent? I bet you will make someone happy if you share your talent!

Mashell swam home to Momma Mermaid. Mashell looked at Momma, whose eyes were weary. The twins were screaming as loud as a whale. *"Waaaaaaaaaaa!"* They were fighting over Floppy, their toy fishy. Mashell saw how tired Momma was and hesitated to sing. She thought to herself that she didn't want to make more noise for Momma. She thought about how much she enjoyed singing and it occurred to her that maybe, just maybe, Momma would enjoy listening to her sing. Her tail shook (can you shake your legs like a tail?), but she went for it! She decided to be brave and shine like a starfish. With a big "SWISH" she went for it and sang!

"La La La La La La La!" Mashell sang as loud and strong as her gills would let her. Then she saw Momma smile, so she sang louder and as beautifully as she could, showing her unique talent. *"La La La La La!"*

Momma Mermaid's tail was glowing bright pink. She was overjoyed by the talent that Mashell had shared. Double and Trouble liked it too. When Mashell switched to a soft ballad, they fell asleep to the sweet sound of her voice. Mashell was so happy that her tail beamed bright purple.

Momma Mermaid hugged Mashell and said to her, *"I am so proud of you for sharing your talent and facing your fear."*

Mashell shared her talent even though she was afraid to do it and it made her entire family happy. Can you bring out your mermaid strength and share your talent? If you get shy, try being brave and going for it anyway. Believing in yourself is the first step to reaching any goal. Soon you will be on your way to achieving your wildest dreams!

When you are told you can't,
close your eyes and believe you can.

This is a wishing mirror. Draw a picture of who you wish to be and the place you dream of living. When I colored in my mirror, I drew myself as a mermaid, swimming in the Pacific Ocean near the Hawaiian Islands. When you are done coloring your dream mirror, tape it on your bedroom wall next to your light switch. Every time you turn your light on, you will be lighting up your dream. If you can see your dream, you will be closer to making your dream real!

There is time to
be in the moment,
time to be evolving,
and time to reflect.
Balancing them
will lead to
happiness.

In this image you will be connecting the dots. Take a pencil or pen and draw a line to connect the dots. Do you see an outline of a mermaid with a big tail? Once you see the mermaid, color in the tail how you imagine your own mermaid tail would look. What would it look like? What colors would your tail be?

Mermaid *Kariel* ©

When you feel different from everyone else, know that it's because you have something special to offer them.

Wishing Mirror

This is a magic mirror. Write all of the things you dream of being someday. For example, I wrote on my mirror these things: "I will be a real mermaid. I will always be honest. I will always be kind. I will have lots of good friends. I will live in Hawaii. I will be a children's book author and illustrator." Now you write things that you really want to do, to happen, or to be like. Once you have everything written on your magic mirror, cut out this page and tape it to your bathroom mirror. Every morning when you brush your teeth, you will need to read what you wrote. In time, you will start to make your dreams come true.

Rest is important.
It gives your mind
the time to create.

Mermaid Kariel's baby by Lisa Hoang

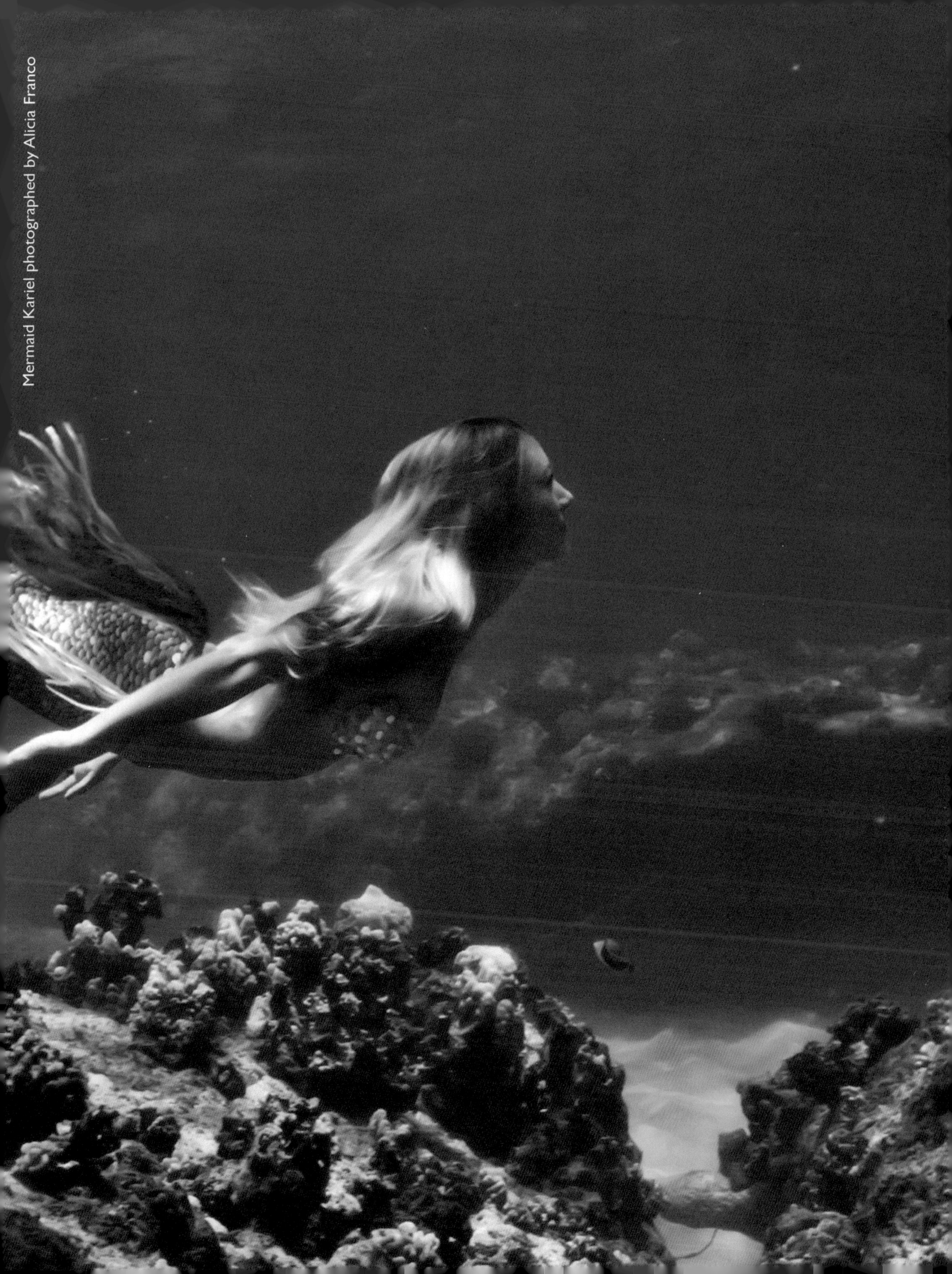

Mermaid Kariel photographed by Alicia Franco

Mermaid Kariel photographed by Wyland The Artist

Share your heart

Mermaid Kariel photographed by Alicia Franco

A photo of you and me

Be the light in your own life